PuRRmaids

14

Contest Cat-tastrophe

by Sudipta Bardhan-Quallen

illustrations by Vivien Wu

A STEPPING STONE BOOK™

Random House 🏠 New York

Text copyright © 2023 by Sudipta Bardhan-Quallen
Cover art copyright © 2023 by Andrew Farley
Interior illustrations copyright © 2023 by Vivien Wu

Visit us on the Web!
rhcbooks.com

Educators and librarians, for a variety of teaching tools, visit us at
RHTeachersLibrarians.com

Library of Congress Cataloging-in-Publication Data is available upon request.
ISBN 978-0-593-64537-6 (trade)—ISBN 978-0-593-64538-3 (lib. bdg.)—
ISBN 978-0-593-64539-0 (ebook)

Printed in the United States of America
10 9 8 7 6 5 4 3 2 1
First Edition

This book has been officially leveled by using
the F&P Text Level Gradient™ Leveling System.

Random House Children's Books supports the
First Amendment and celebrates the right to read.

To Miss Izzy's kids

1

In Room Eel-Twelve of sea school, a black-and-white purrmaid named Angel listened to the day's lesson. Angel loved her class. She loved her teacher, Ms. Harbor. Every day was a new adventure.

But just because she loved sea school didn't mean that Angel didn't think being out of school was fin-tastic, too! It was the last lesson before the weekend. Angel was very eager for the final bell to ring. She kept playing with her friendship bracelet, waiting for the minutes to tick by. Angel's bracelet matched the ones Coral and Shelly wore. They had been best friends fur-ever, and they used the charms on their bracelets to remind them of all the fun they'd had together.

Luckily, Angel wasn't the only one sneaking peeks at the time. Shelly kept pretending to see dirt on her shoulder. She hated it if anything got on her silky,

white fur! When she brushed it off with her paw, Shelly turned her head—toward the clock!

Coral almost always paid complete attention to Ms. Harbor. *Almost* always. This afternoon, the little orange kitten seemed to be stretching her paws a lot. Every time she stretched, she twisted to face the clock!

"I think we should end the lesson early," Ms. Harbor finally said. "You all

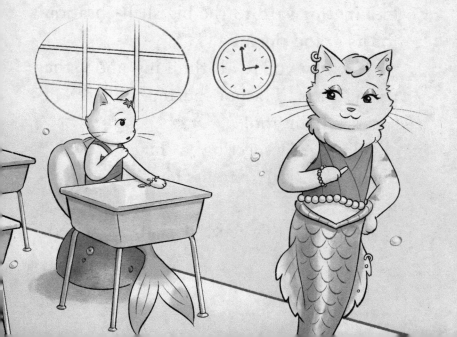

seem like you're thinking about something else."

"We're sorry," the students said.

"It's just that we're all so excited!" Angel exclaimed. "It's almost time!"

"The doors might already be open!" Baker said.

"I doubt it," Taylor replied. "They're keeping it a secret until tomorrow."

The *it* was the Kittentail Cove Library's new reading room. Everyone in town was looking forward to the big shell-ebration for its grand opening!

"I know you're all thinking about the party," Ms. Harbor purred. "Here's a secret—I am, too!"

"They're expecting a huge crowd," Shelly said. "My parents have been cooking all week."

"Yum! I can't wait!" Coral exclaimed.

"Paw-some books, paw-some food, and a big new space! Who could ask for more?"

"But there *will* be more!" Adrianna said. "A new librarian and a contest and prizes . . ."

Angel leaned over to whisper to Coral and Shelly. "Adrianna's right. Prizes make everything better!"

"Can anyone guess my favorite part of the new reading room?" Ms. Harbor asked.

"All the new books?" Shelly asked.

"The comfy seats?" Umiko asked.

"A place where we can do homework for hours?" Coral asked.

"Coral!" Baker hissed. "Don't mention homework!"

"She hasn't given us any yet," Taylor added. "Don't remind her!"

Ms. Harbor chuckled. "Don't worry.

There's no homework tonight. Those were all good guesses. But none of those is my favorite part."

"What is it?" Cascade asked.

"A reading room is a place to share stories," Ms. Harbor answered. "You can discuss books with friends. You can make new friends over the stories you discover. It's a place to learn, grow, and become a better friend." She grinned. "It's also a purr-fect reason to have a party! You'll definitely see me there. I'll be at the library later this afternoon and bright and early tomorrow. There is still a lot of work to do, and I'm a volunteer."

"Work?" Angel asked. "Parties are supposed to be fun, not work!"

"Having fun takes a lot of work!" Ms. Harbor replied. "But don't worry. The volunteers for the shell-ebration are going to make sure that all you have to do is show up and enjoy."

I'm good at that! Angel thought.

Every day after sea school, Angel, Shelly, and Coral headed home together. They swam down Canal Street, past the Kittentail Cove Library, straight toward Leondra's Square.

Today, though, the three kittens stopped when they reached the library. After sea school, the library was one of Angel's favorite places in town. Coral and Shelly loved the library, too—but for different reasons. Angel loved books about unusual animals and stories of adventure. Shelly loved cookbooks and books about music. And Coral loved . . . everything!

Coral was happy with a book in her paws, no matter what it was about.

Outside the library, the girls saw purrmaids wearing hard hats and vests that said CASPIAN CONSTRUCTION. They

were in charge of building the new reading room.

"There's Mr. Caspian's construction crew," Coral said. "They're packing up their tools."

"I guess they're finishing up," Angel purred.

"I really wish we could see the reading room today," Shelly said.

Angel agreed. She liked surprises—but she didn't like waiting for them! "I know the grand opening is tomorrow," she said, "but it can't hurt to take a quick peek."

"Maybe we'll get lucky!" Shelly exclaimed.

2

Angel, Shelly, and Coral hurried into the library. Angel said, "Let's check the reading room. Last one there is a rotten skeg!"

The girls swam toward a doorway in the back wall. Someone was floating through it. He pulled the door closed with one paw and put a hammer in his tool belt with the other.

"Mr. Caspian!" Coral shouted. "Don't close that door!"

Mr. Caspian turned toward the girls. He smiled when he recognized them. "You know I can't leave it open, Coral," he replied.

"Can't we just take a quick peek?" Angel asked.

"Please?" Shelly added.

Mr. Caspian chuckled. "That wouldn't be fair, girls!"

Angel sighed. "I guess you're right," she said.

"Don't look so disappointed," Mr. Caspian said. "It's only a little longer before the doors open tomorrow."

"That's going to feel like fur-ever!" Coral moaned.

"Well," Mr. Caspian purred, winking, "I can't give you a sneak peek of the reading room. But I can give you a sneak peek of something else."

"What else is there?" Shelly asked.

"Would you like to meet the new librarian?" Mr. Caspian asked.

"Yes!" all three purrmaids exclaimed at the same time.

Mr. Caspian waved for the girls to follow him. "Come on, then!"

Kittentail Cove Library's new librarian was Mrs. Bluefin. Angel knew that because there was a sign on the main desk. But she didn't know anything else about her.

Mr. Caspian led the girls to Mrs. Bluefin's office. "There she is," he said, pointing through the door.

Angel noticed two things right away. First, Mrs. Bluefin was beautiful. She had silky, white fur with black and orange spots. She also had the biggest, bluest eyes that Angel had ever seen. She wore a long blue dress that matched her eyes.

The second thing Angel noticed was a stack of flyers in Mrs. Bluefin's paws. She was too far away to read everything on the top sheet, but she could see two words from across the room: *contest* and *prizes*.

This is going to be fin-teresting! Angel thought.

Mr. Caspian purred, "Hello, Mrs. Bluefin."

Mrs. Bluefin looked up. "Hello there!" she replied. "It's nice to see you, Mr. Caspian. Can I help you with something?"

Mr. Caspian grinned. "You don't start working until tomorrow!" he said.

"You're right," Mrs. Bluefin answered. "But a librarian is always here to help!" She turned toward Angel, Coral, and Shelly. "Would you girls like to introduce yourselves?"

"I'm Shelly," Shelly said. "This is Angel. And this is Coral." She pointed to the others.

"The girls wanted to meet you," Mr. Caspian said, "so I brought them by before I finished up for the day." He waved goodbye. "I'll see you all at the shell-ebration!"

"Are you girls excited about tomorrow?" Mrs. Bluefin asked. She hung a flyer on her door as she talked.

Angel nodded. "I love parties!"

"I think it's going to be paw-some!" Mrs. Bluefin said. "But there's still a lot of work to do!"

"Can we help?" Shelly asked.

Mrs. Bluefin thought for a moment. "Not right now. But if you can come early tomorrow, one of the volunteers might need a paw. Do you girls know Ms. Harbor?"

"She's our teacher!" Coral exclaimed.

"My daughter is joining Ms. Harbor's class next week!" Mrs. Bluefin said.

"We'll find Ms. Harbor before the shell-ebration begins," Angel said. "If she needs any help, we'll do our best!"

"Purr-fect!" Mrs. Bluefin replied. "Now I'd better get back to hanging these up around the library."

When Coral and Shelly started to follow Mrs. Bluefin down the hall, Angel grabbed their paws. "Wait. Did you see this?" She pointed to the door.

CONTEST

The Kittentail Cove Library is very excited about our new reading room, the Fanta-sea Lounge. But we need help decorating! So we're hosting a contest. Create a paw-some poster about reading—something that will get everyone inspired to pick up a book!

Register at the main desk to enter.
FIRST PRIZE: The poster with the most votes will be hung in the library!
SECOND and **THIRD PRIZES:** to be announced

Contest Committee: Mrs. Bluefin, Ms. Harbor, and Mr. Caspian

3

"The Fanta-sea Lounge," Coral said. "What a great name!"

"It is, but did you see the art contest?" Angel asked. "I didn't know about that one. I love art!"

"It's more than an art contest," Shelly said. "It needs to inspire purrmaids to read."

"And I love reading!" Coral added. "It would be fin-credible to make something that would be hung up in the library. I'd love it here even more than I already do!"

"I agree!" Angel said. "At least one of us has to win a prize tomorrow. The art contest might be our best bet. Let's sign up and get to work on our posters!"

Angel smiled at her friends. But for some reason, they didn't smile back. "Is something wrong?" Angel asked.

"Well," Shelly purred, "I don't know if I'll have time to make a poster tonight. I have to help my parents get all the food ready for the shell-ebration."

"That makes sense," Angel said, nodding. "How about you, Coral? Do you want to come with me so we can sign up?"

Coral bit her lip. "I don't know if I should make a poster. Not if you're making one."

"Why not?" Angel asked.

"Because you're so good at art!" Coral replied. "I can't make anything better than you."

"That's not true," Angel said. She floated closer to Coral. "You're really good at art, too. And like you said—this is more than an art contest. It's about reading, too. And you know more about reading than anyone I know!"

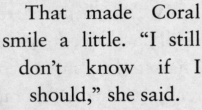

That made Coral smile a little. "I still don't know if I should," she said.

"Why don't we go to the main desk?" Shelly suggested. "Angel can sign up, and Coral can think about it along the way."

Coral nodded.

As the girls swam toward the main desk, Angel realized something. *Coral really, really wants to win the poster contest.* She thought about what Ms. Harbor had said about reading rooms helping you become a better friend. *I really love art.* She frowned. *But would I be a better friend if I don't sign up to compete against Coral? What should I do?*

Angel had her mind on Coral and the poster contest. She wasn't paying attention to where she was swimming. Not until she bumped into someone!

"Oof!" said the other purrmaid. Angel had knocked her down to the floor.

Angel had never seen the other purrmaid before. She had white fur with orange spots, and she looked like she was Angel's age. She had been holding a box of starfish decorations. When Angel bumped into her, the box of decorations spilled everywhere.

"I am so sorry!" Angel exclaimed. "Let me help you up." She held out her paw and helped the other girl up. She noticed the girl was wearing a bracelet of blue beads. "That's a beautiful bracelet," Angel said. "I've never seen beads like that."

"Thank you," the girl said.

"I'll pick up these starfish with you," Angel said. She grabbed a pawful of decorations. "I don't think we know each other, do we?"

The girl said, "We just moved here."

"I'm Angel," Angel said. "What's your name?"

But before the girl could answer, Shelly shouted, "Angel! Ms. Harbor is here!"

"Coming!" Angel replied. She said to the girl, "I'll be right back!" She hurried away.

When Angel reached her friends, they were already talking to Ms. Harbor. "I'm just not sure I should sign up for the contest," Coral said. "There are purrmaids who are better artists."

"I don't know if that's true," Ms. Harbor purred. "I love your artwork."

"That's what I told her," Angel said.

"You could always sign up today," Ms. Harbor said. "Then if you change your mind, you don't have to enter your poster. But you could think about it all night."

"That's a good plan," Coral agreed.

"Let's do it!" Angel exclaimed.

Angel and Coral swam to the sign-up sheet. There were already a lot of names on it. Angel added her name first. Then Coral wrote hers.

The girls floated back toward Shelly. "Ms. Harbor had to go," Shelly said. "She had to talk to Mrs. Bluefin about something."

All of a sudden, Angel remembered the new girl. *I told her I'd be right back!* She looked around to try to find her. But the new girl was gone. *And she must have picked up all the decorations by herself!*

4

"Oh no!" Angel moaned. "I completely fur-got!"

"Fur-got what?" Coral asked.

"I knocked someone over earlier," Angel continued. "All her decorations spilled, and I was going to help her clean up after I said hello to Ms. Harbor. But then we started talking and went to sign up for the contest. And I fur-got about her." She frowned. "I left before she even told me her name!"

"Maybe she's still here somewhere," Coral said.

"I would help you look for her," Shelly said, "but I have to get home."

"To make your special shrimp salad?" Angel joked.

"I get hungry just thinking about it!" Coral purred.

"I'll make sure to save you some," Shelly said.

After one quick group hug, Shelly left. Then Coral said, "I was going to look for ideas for my poster. But I can help you instead."

"The library is closing soon," Angel said. "We don't have a lot of time. You should look for ideas. I'll try to find the girl."

"Purr-fect," Coral agreed. "I'm going to the fairy tale section."

Angel nodded. "I'll find you there soon," she said.

Angel swam up and down the library aisles. She saw some of her classmates. She saw more poster-contest flyers. But the new girl wasn't anywhere. *She might think I was being mean to her on purpose,* she thought. Angel felt paw-ful!

Before Angel knew it, a librarian announced that the library was closing in ten minutes.

I hope I'll see the girl here tomorrow, Angel thought. *Then I can apologize.*

Angel began to look for Coral. That's when she saw Ms. Harbor. *Maybe she's seen the new girl,* Angel thought.

But Ms. Harbor was talking on her shell phone. She was frowning. When she hung up, Angel asked, "What's wrong?"

"That was Mr. Shippley," Ms. Harbor replied.

"Is he all right?" Angel asked. Mr. Shippley was the librarian at sea school. He always helped Angel pick a purr-fect book to check out.

Ms. Harbor nodded. "Mr. Shippley is resting. He isn't feeling well enough to come to the shell-ebration, though. But Mrs. Bluefin decided she can't count the votes. Her daughter is entering the contest, so she thinks it's best for others to take charge of the votes."

That made sense to Angel.

"That means we're missing someone on the contest committee," Ms. Harbor continued. "I was hoping Mr. Shippley could help, but I guess I have to make a few more calls."

Angel frowned. "Could someone else volunteer?" she asked.

Ms. Harbor shrugged. "I hope so!"

Angel thought for a moment. *Ms. Harbor has helped me with so many things this year. Maybe I could help her now.* She said, "I could be on the committee, Ms. Harbor."

"That would be paw-some!" Ms. Harbor exclaimed, grinning. But then her grin disappeared. "Angel, volunteers on the contest committee shouldn't count their own votes. That might look unfair to other contestants. Do you understand that being a volunteer means you can't enter the contest?"

Angel bit her lip. She hadn't thought about that.

"It's all right if you don't want to volunteer," Ms. Harbor purred. "I know you love art."

Angel thought about how much Coral

wanted to win this contest. *Coral would feel better if her poster wasn't competing with mine. I wasn't very thoughtful when I didn't go back to help that girl before. But I can be thoughtful toward one of my best friends now.* She turned to Ms. Harbor and said, "I *do* love art. But I love helping, too. So I'm ready to dive in!"

"Fin-tastic!" Ms. Harbor cheered.

"What's fin-tastic?" Coral asked. She swam up behind Angel.

"Coral!" Angel said. "I was about to go find you."

"I know," Coral said. "But I heard your voices so I thought I'd come to you instead. Now tell me. What's fin-tastic?"

"Angel has joined the poster-contest committee," Ms. Harbor replied.

Coral frowned. "Does that mean she's going to be one of the judges?"

Ms. Harbor shook her head. "We're not judging the entries. The contest committee just counts the votes."

"That's good," Coral said. "It wouldn't be fair if someone got to enter the contest *and* judge the posters."

"Actually," Angel said, "I'm not going to enter the contest."

"Why not?" Coral asked.

"Because I'd be counting my own votes," Angel explained. "And that wouldn't be fair."

"But you would never do anything sneaky," Coral said.

"I agree, Coral," Ms. Harbor said. "But, just in case, the purrmaids on the contest committee shouldn't enter the contest."

"It's really nice of you to volunteer, Angel," Coral said, "even though that means you can't be in the poster contest. I know you really wanted to win a prize."

"Well, I'll just keep my claws crossed for you to win!" Angel said, grinning. *And for the girl I met to be here tomorrow!*

5

Angel and Mommy left for the shell-ebration first thing in the morning. "I can't believe you're up this early," Mommy said, yawning.

"I'm too excited to sleep!" Angel replied, grabbing Mommy's paw to drag her faster. "I can't wait to see the Fanta-sea Lounge. And Coral's poster. And all the other posters—"

"All right, all right!" Mommy cried.

"Since I'm on the contest committee, there might be things that I need to do before the party starts," Angel continued. *It would have been nice to compete in the art contest,* she thought. But being on the contest committee was a big responsibility. That made Angel feel important. And she liked that feeling!

There were some purrmaids outside the library already, even though it was early. Angel saw Shelly's parents, Mr. and Mrs. Lake. "Can I go see if Shelly is here, Mommy?" Angel asked.

"Of course," Mommy answered. She pointed to a purrmaid in a top hat floating in front of the library. "I see Mayor Rivers over there. I'm going to help him set up."

Angel swam toward the Lake family. She could smell the delicious food before she even reached them.

"Good morning, Angel," Mrs. Lake called.

"You're up early!" Mr. Lake added. "We heard you joined the poster-contest committee."

Angel nodded. "I did!"

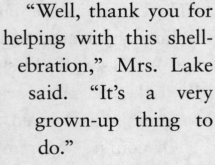

"Well, thank you for helping with this shell-ebration," Mrs. Lake said. "It's a very grown-up thing to do."

Angel grinned. "Thank you!" Then she asked, "Is Shelly around?"

"She is," Mr. Lake

replied. "She's bringing us some trays of sushi from our cart."

"I'll go help," Angel purred. "It'll get done twice as fast."

"Then Shelly can join you twice as quickly!" Mrs. Lake said. "She did so much work last night, we told her she could go enjoy the shell-ebration as soon as all the sushi is set out."

Angel found Shelly taking a tray out of the Lake Restaurant cart. "I'm here to give you a paw!" she announced.

Shelly smiled. "Your timing is purr-fect! I only have two trays left."

"And then you're free to party!" Angel exclaimed. She began to pick up the last tray. "Oof! This is heavy!"

"Really?" Shelly asked. "I didn't think so."

"I know how to fix this," Angel said.

She picked up a piece of sushi and plopped it into her mouth. "Now it's not too heavy anymore!"

The girls giggled as they swam back to the food table. They waved goodbye to Shelly's parents—after Angel had one more snack!

Most of Kittentail Cove had come to the library. Angel looked through the crowd. "Is Coral here yet?"

Shelly shrugged. "I haven't seen her."

"She's always early for everything," Angel said. She scratched her head. "I'm surprised she isn't here before us."

"The shell-ebration doesn't start for another hour," Shelly said. "Coral will be here soon."

"I hope so," Angel said. She pointed to the library door. "I should join the contest committee. Maybe we have responsibilities already."

"I'll keep looking for Coral," Shelly

said. "Then we'll meet inside for the grand opening."

Angel nodded. "See you soon!"

Mommy and Mayor Rivers were floating right inside the library doors. Most days, no matter how loud it was outside, everyone hushed as soon as they swam through the doors. Angel usually had a purr-oblem staying quiet. She always seemed to have something to say!

But on a day like this, Angel didn't have to try her best to *shhhh*! It was paw-sitively packed inside the library! Everyone seemed to be chattering. It was the loudest the library had ever been!

"I'm glad I don't have to keep my voice down," Angel said.

"Oh, Angel," Mommy teased, "you never keep your voice down."

Angel stuck her tongue out while Mommy giggled.

"I love everything you say," Mommy purred. "You know that."

Angel squeezed Mommy's paw and smiled. Then Mommy handed her a piece of paper. "This is your ballot for the poster contest," Mommy said. "Everyone gets one."

"One, and only one!" Mayor Rivers added.

"Am I allowed to vote?" Angel asked. "Since I'm on the contest committee?"

"Of course you are," Mommy replied. "Your opinion is just as valuable as anyone else's. That's only fair."

"Yay!" Angel exclaimed. She took her ballot and put it in her pocket. "Time to do my important job!"

6

Ms. Harbor and Mr. Caspian were floating outside the door to the reading room. They had a table set up, and some purrmaids were bringing them posters. Mr. Caspian was hanging one of the posters on the wall.

Angel swam over and asked, "Can I help?"

"Purr-fect timing!" Ms. Harbor said. "I need to put up these signs so everyone knows where to find the poster contest"—she patted the ballot box—"and where to cast their ballots. Mr. Caspian is putting the posters on the wall so everyone can see them. We need you to give every poster a number and to match that number to the artist's name."

"I can do that!" Angel purred.

Ms. Harbor handed Angel a piece of paper. "These are all the purrmaids who registered for the contest."

Six of the names already had numbers next to them. "Those are the posters I've hung up so far," Mr. Caspian said.

There were thirty names on the registration list. Angel crossed out her own name. "I won't be entering," she said. "So we don't need to worry about this one." Angel did some quick math in her head. Thirty minus one is twenty-nine. Twenty-nine minus six is twenty-three. "We are waiting for twenty-three more posters."

"I hope I brought enough nails!" Mr. Caspian said, laughing.

Angel floated in front of the display wall. As posters came in, she gave them a number and Mr. Caspian hung them up.

Before long, there were twenty-eight posters on the wall.

"Is that all of them?" Mr. Caspian asked.

Angel shook her head. "There should be one more." *Whose poster is missing?* she wondered. She checked the list. Then she gulped. The only purrmaid who hadn't brought them a poster was Coral!

Right then, Mrs. Bluefin made an announcement over the library's speakers. "If you still have a poster for the contest, please bring it to the contest committee at the display wall. Entries will close in five minutes so we can all enjoy the grand opening of the Fanta-sea Lounge!"

Angel felt butterfly fish fluttering in her tummy. *Where is Coral?* she thought.

More and more purrmaids floated into the library. They began to crowd around the door to the Fanta-sea Lounge. But still, Angel couldn't see Coral.

Mrs. Bluefin had moved to float in front of the closed door. *That means Coral is almost out of time!* Angel thought.

Then someone tapped Angel's shoulder. Angel was so surprised she almost yelped. When she turned to see who it was, she *did* yelp! "Coral! I've been looking for you!"

"I was finishing my poster," Coral replied. "I worked on it until the last minute."

"The very last minute!" Shelly added. "It was too crowded to come in through the front door. We never would have reached you."

"So I helped them through the side entrance," Mrs. Lake said. "The library lets us use it when we're delivering food. I thought we could make an exception today!"

"Let's get this on the wall," Angel said, taking it from Coral. "Mr. Caspian, can you hang up one last poster?"

"You're just in time, Coral," Mr. Caspian said. "Mrs. Bluefin is about to open the door to the Fanta-sea Lounge. And I have one nail left!"

Coral grinned as Mr. Caspian hung

her poster. Angel labeled it with a number. "You're lucky number twenty-nine, Coral," she said. "I can't wait to vote for you!"

"Me too," Shelly said.

"Me three," Coral added. "Except . . . we didn't get ballots yet!"

"I'll make sure you get ballots in a minute," Angel said. "First, we need to see the Fanta-sea Lounge!"

7

It was lucky that the door to the reading room was next to the display wall. That meant Angel, Shelly, and Coral would be some of the first purrmaids to see the new lounge!

"Welcome, everyone," Mrs. Bluefin purred. "I can't wait to show you our brand-new reading room."

"Then show us already!" someone shouted from the crowd.

Mrs. Bluefin grinned. "Would you please count down from three?"

The crowd shouted, "Three . . . two . . . one!"

Mrs. Bluefin pushed the door open. "Welcome to the Fanta-sea Lounge!" she shouted.

It was more clam-azing inside than anyone had guessed!

Mrs. Bluefin guided everyone through the different sections of the Fanta-sea Lounge. "This is the Enchanted Ocean," she said. There was a group of big, cushy chairs made from toadstool corals.

"This section is called Books at the Beach," Mrs. Bluefin continued. There, Mr. Caspian's workers had built pillars that looked like palm trees. Hammocks hung between the trees.

"I've saved the best for last," Mrs.

Bluefin said. "The Tails and Tales Theater!"

"Beautiful," Coral whispered.

"This stage will be great for story-time," Mrs. Bluefin said. "And the sea-grass carpets are purr-fect for sitting on."

Then she pointed to the empty wall above the stage. "Best of all, the winning poster from our contest will be hung right there. In fact, would the members of our contest committee please come up here to tell everyone about the poster contest?"

The crowd began to clap. Coral and Shelly pushed Angel forward. "Go ahead," Shelly whispered.

Angel smiled and joined Ms. Harbor and Mr. Caspian. "Many of our talented Kittentail Cove artists created beautiful posters to help inspire us all to pick up a book," Ms. Harbor announced. "They are hung on the wall outside this room. Please take a moment to look at them and cast a vote for your favorite."

"There are numbers on all the posters for you to mark on your ballot," Angel said. "You can put your ballots in the box on the table next to the display wall when you're done."

"If you didn't get a ballot yet," Ms. Harbor said, "we have more on the table."

"Just remember," Mr. Caspian added, "only one vote per purrmaid!"

"The votes will be counted in one hour," Mrs. Bluefin said. "So get your ballot in soon. In the meantime, feel free to explore the Fanta-sea Lounge."

"Don't fur-get to grab a yummy snack!" Angel added. "The sushi from the Lake Restaurant is really good!"

"What should we do first?" Shelly asked.

Angel knew exactly where they should go. "Let's vote!"

"We haven't had a chance to look at all the posters yet," Coral said.

Angel's eyes grew wide. "You know we've all decided who to vote for, right?" she asked.

Coral grinned. "I hope you'll vote for me. But we should look at everyone else's work."

"I agree with Coral," Shelly said. "Just because we have a favorite doesn't mean there aren't other nice posters!"

The girls swam toward the display wall. Mr. Caspian was floating in front of the ballot box, keeping an eye on it.

Angel realized that she barely looked at the posters when she was checking them in. She was too busy making sure they got the right numbers. Now she had a chance to see how they were all beautiful in their own way.

Of course, Angel loved Coral's poster. It showed a purrmaid diving down into deep water. The bubbles floating off her body were actually book covers. Looking closely at the ocean floor in the poster, Angel saw that it was stacks and stacks of books. It said DIVE INTO AN OCEAN OF BOOKS.

"Wow! This is brilliant, Coral," Angel said.

Coral grinned. "Thank you! I hope other purrmaids think so, too."

"I think they will," Shelly purred.

There were two more posters Angel really liked. One of them showed a purrmaid splashing her tail against the ocean. Instead of water drops flying everywhere, the splash threw up a spray of books. It said MAKE A SPLASH WITH A FIN-TASTIC TALE.

The other poster Angel liked said FLIP INTO THE PAGES OF A PAW-SOME FANTA-SEA. It showed a purrmaid with an open book. The pages were being flipped, and there were all sorts of characters coming out from between the pages. Angel

4

saw dolphins, sea turtles, humans, and even a mermicorn!

As nice as those posters were, Angel was still going to vote for number twenty-nine. She filled out her ballot and held it up. "I'm ready to vote. How about you?"

Shelly and Coral grinned. "Ready!" they both answered.

The girls put their ballots in the box. Then Angel exclaimed, "Let's join the party!"

8

Inside and outside the library, there really was so much to do! The girls ran a book relay. Shelly began at the starting line, holding a copy of *The Great Cats-by*. She swam to Coral and passed the book to her. Then Coral raced toward Angel. Angel got the book from Coral and darted toward the finish line. She swam as quickly as she could, but Umiko was just a little faster.

Shelly and Coral met Angel at the finish line. "That was fun," Shelly said, "even though the Catfish Club beat us."

"Their book wasn't as heavy as ours, though," Angel replied, pointing to their copy of *Where the Wild Things Swim*.

"We'll choose a lighter book next time!" Coral said, giggling.

The purrmaids floated over to the dance floor. They learned the Book Boogie. Then they watched Mayor Rivers do his favorite magic trick. "Right before your eyes," he said, "I'm going to make this sushi disappear!" It was silly, but everyone loved it.

Angel didn't realize how much time had passed. Suddenly, Mrs. Bluefin's voice came out of the speakers. "Would the members of the poster-contest committee please meet in Mrs. Bluefin's office to count the votes?"

"I guess it's time for me to get to work," Angel said.

"We can't wait to hear who won!" Coral said.

"I hope it'll be you!" Angel replied.

Angel reached Mrs. Bluefin's office as Mr. Caspian was swimming up, holding the ballot box. "It's heavy," he said. "I think there are a lot of votes to count!"

Ms. Harbor said, "Let's take the ballots out and put them on the desk. Then we can sort them and count them."

Mr. Caspian dumped the ballots out onto the desk.

"Be careful!" Angel said. "We don't want to lose any votes!"

Mr. Caspian frowned. "I wasn't thinking," he said. He took a quick look on the ground around the desk. "I think they're all here."

"You got lucky," Ms. Harbor said. "We should get to work. Everyone wants to know who won!"

The three purrmaids unfolded the ballots. Then they sorted them into twenty-nine stacks. Ms. Harbor counted the ballots in each stack and wrote them out on a piece of paper. Then she asked, "Could you two double-check my totals?"

Angel grinned. "Ms. Harbor! I'm sure you're very good at counting!"

"Thank you, Angel," Ms. Harbor purred, winking. "But we want to be completely fair. Double- and triple-checking will make sure that there are no mistakes."

"She's right," Mr. Caspian said.

After all the extra checking, they had the final vote count. "It looks like we have thirty-one votes for entry number four," Ms. Harbor said. "Seventeen votes for number twenty-six. And thirty-three votes for number twenty-nine."

Angel did a twirl in the water. Number twenty-nine was Coral's poster! "We have a winner!" she exclaimed.

"Yes, we do," Ms. Harbor said. "I'll let Mrs. Bluefin know so she can make an announcement."

"And I'll take the posters off the wall," Mr. Caspian added. "That way, we can show the winner when we make the announcement."

Ms. Harbor and Mr. Caspian swam away. Angel decided to clean up. She stuffed the ballots back into the box. Then she noticed something. A small stack of ballots had fallen behind the desk, onto Mrs. Bluefin's chair. She leaned down and picked them up. *They must have fallen when Mr. Caspian dumped the ballot box*, she thought. *That means we haven't counted them.*

Angel was about to shout for Ms. Harbor. But she stopped. *Coral is winning right now*, she thought. These ballots were still folded. Angel couldn't tell if they were votes for Coral's poster or not. *If I never saw them, no one would know.* Angel bit her lip. *What should I do?*

9

Angel hadn't made a decision yet. But she heard someone coming. So she quickly tucked the uncounted ballots into her pocket and spun around.

"We were looking for you, Angel," Shelly said as she swam into the office. Coral followed her closely.

"We saw Ms. Harbor," Coral added. "She said the ballots were counted so you could come hang out with us now."

Not all of them, Angel thought. But her friends didn't know that.

"Are you going to come back to the party?" Shelly asked.

"Umm," Angel replied. "Sure. Yes, I'm coming."

Another announcement came out of the speakers. "The poster-contest winners will be revealed very soon in the Tails and Tales Theater."

Coral's eyes grew wide. "It's almost time!" she purred.

"We have to hurry!" Shelly added. She was almost as excited as Coral was.

Angel had butterfly fish in her tummy. She felt in her pocket for the uncounted ballots. *I only have to keep this secret for a little while longer,* she thought. *Then I never have to think of it again!* "Let's go, I guess," she said.

Angel thought her friends would be too focused on the contest to notice anything wrong. But that's not the kind of friends Coral and Shelly were! Her friends looked at each other for a moment. Then, before Angel left the office, Coral grabbed her paw. Shelly swam around and shut the door.

"All right, Angel," Shelly said. "We can see something is wrong. Can you please tell us?"

Angel looked down at her tail. She didn't know what to say.

"Is it because I made you feel like you couldn't enter the contest?" Coral asked softly. "I'm so sorry about that. I wish I hadn't done it."

"No, I'm not upset about that at all!" Angel replied. "I'm happy that I helped you feel better about entering. Because your poster is paw-some!"

"Is it because Coral didn't win?" Shelly asked. "Is that why you're upset?"

When Angel still didn't say anything, Coral said, "Because it doesn't matter to me if I won. I'm just glad you pushed me to enter."

Angel sighed. "No, that's not it," she said. "Coral got the most votes in the ballots that we counted."

"Then what is it?" Shelly asked.

"After we counted everything," Angel said, "Ms. Harbor left to find Mrs. Bluefin. That's when I found these." She reached into her pocket and took out the ballots. "They must have fallen out. They haven't been counted yet. I don't know if these would change the winner."

Coral gasped. "You have to give these to Ms. Harbor!"

"But what if this ruins it for you, Coral?" Angel asked. "It would be all my fault!"

"I want Coral to win, too," Shelly said. "But it wouldn't be fair not to count all the votes."

"And I don't want to win by cheating," Coral said. She put a paw around Angel's waist. "You're a good friend for trying to support me."

"But this isn't really supporting you, is

it?" Angel said, sighing. "It really wouldn't be fair." She knew what she had to do.

Just then, they heard Mrs. Bluefin's voice again. "Contest winners will be announced in fifteen minutes."

Angel's eyes grew wide. "We don't have a lot of time to fix this!"

The three girls rushed out of Mrs. Bluefin's office. They raced toward the Fanta-sea Lounge. Angel was in the lead, which is why she was the one who bumped into someone. And she sent that someone tumbling to the floor.

"Ouch!" the someone yelled.

That's when Angel realized who the purrmaid was. It was the new girl! Angel had knocked into her again!

"I'm so sorry!" Angel exclaimed. "You must think this is just how I say hello. I can't believe I did this to you again!"

"It's all right," the new girl purred. Then she frowned. "I think my bracelet broke when I fell." She held up her paw. There was a broken string with a few bright blue beads left on it. There were more blue beads on the floor.

Angel stopped for a moment. "I really want to help you," she said. "But I can't right now. I have to get these ballots to Ms. Harbor or they won't get counted in time!"

Coral waved Angel off. "Go, Angel. There's no time to lose."

Shelly held a paw out to the new girl to help her up. "We'll get this cleaned up."

Angel nodded and raced away. *I hope I'm not too late!*

10

Ms. Harbor was floating near the Fanta-sea Lounge door. Angel raced toward her. "Ms. Harbor!" she exclaimed.

"What's the matter, Angel?" Ms. Harbor asked.

Angel held up the ballots. "Mrs. Bluefin can't announce the winner yet," she said. "These haven't been counted."

Ms. Harbor's eyes grew wide. "Where did those come from?"

"I found them on the chair," Angel replied. "They must have fallen off the desk. We only checked the floor, so we didn't see them."

Ms. Harbor grabbed Angel's paw. They pushed their way toward the Tails and Tales Theater. Mrs. Bluefin and Mr. Caspian were facing the crowd at the microphone.

"Excuse me!" Ms. Harbor shouted. She waved her paws around as she and Angel swam down the aisle.

Mrs. Bluefin spotted Ms. Harbor. "Is there a purr-oblem?" she asked. "I was about to announce the winner."

Angel nodded. "There are still votes to count," she said. "We need a few more minutes, please."

The purrmaids in the room began to

whisper. Angel forced herself to ignore them.

"Sorry, everyone," Mrs. Bluefin said into the microphone. "It'll be a little longer before we know who won."

While the crowd groaned, Angel, Ms. Harbor, and Mr. Caspian hurried back to the office. There, Angel held the ballots out to Ms. Harbor. "Here you go," she said. "You and Mr. Caspian can count them."

Ms. Harbor scratched her head. "You're on the contest committee, too, Angel."

Angel looked down at the floor. "I didn't think you could trust me," she mumbled. "I didn't give you the ballots right away."

Ms. Harbor put a paw on Angel's

shoulder. "Maybe you waited a bit to give us the ballots," she purred, "but you *did* give them to us."

"You did the right thing before it was too late," Mr. Caspian added. "That's what matters."

"So let's get counting!" Ms. Harbor said.

🐾 🐾 🐾

In just a few minutes, they had the correct vote counts. "The top three posters are still the top three," Mr. Caspian said. "Thirty-five votes for number four, thirty-four votes for number twenty-nine, and eighteen votes for twenty-six."

Angel looked down at her tail. *Now Coral isn't the winner,* she thought.

"Let's go tell Mrs. Bluefin," Ms. Harbor said.

But Angel shook her head. "Could you two do that? I want to be with Coral when the winner is announced."

"I understand," Ms. Harbor answered.

"We'll see you out there," Mr. Caspian added.

Angel saw Shelly and Coral in the Tails and Tales Theater. There were no empty seats, so they were floating against the back wall. And the new girl was with them!

For the first time, Angel noticed the girl's eyes. They were very beautiful and very blue. Angel had only seen eyes like that once before. "Are you Mrs. Bluefin's daughter?" she asked.

The girl grinned. "Yes," she replied.

"Her name is Cyane," Coral said.

"And she's going to be joining our class next week!" Shelly added.

"That's paw-some!" Angel agreed. Then she said, "I'm sorry I didn't come back sooner to help you yesterday. By the time I looked for you, you were gone. And you'd cleaned up my mess."

"Don't worry," Cyane said. "I had

to go find my mom. I was hoping you wouldn't be mad at me for that!"

"Shhh!" Coral purred. "Mrs. Bluefin is about to make an announcement."

"Coral," Angel whispered, "I have to talk to you."

Coral just squeezed Angel's paw. "You don't have to say anything. It's all right if the votes have changed."

Angel gulped.

From the microphone, Mrs. Bluefin said, "Third prize is a gift certificate for dinner at the Lake Restaurant. The winner is Mrs. Clearwater!"

The crowd cheered. Mrs. Clearwater swam over to get her prize.

"Second prize is," Mrs. Bluefin continued, "a special pass that allows the winner to check out one extra book a month. The winner of this prize is Coral Marsh!"

Mr. Caspian unrolled Coral's poster for everyone to see.

"Wow!" Coral shouted. "I can't believe it!"

"Well, go get your prize!" Shelly exclaimed.

When the cheering quieted down, Mrs. Bluefin said, "The first prize poster, as you know, will hang right here in the Fantasea Lounge. I am so happy to announce the first-prize winner is someone who worked really, really hard on making her poster special. I am so proud of her. First prize goes to Cyane Bluefin!"

Cyane's eyes grew wide. "Did she just say my name?"

"Yes," Angel said, laughing. "And everyone is cheering for you!"

🐾 🐾 🐾

After the announcements, Angel, Coral, and Shelly sunk into the cushy chairs in the Enchanted Ocean. Angel couldn't believe what an exciting day it had turned out to be. "Ms. Harbor was right yesterday," she said. "Having fun takes a lot of work!"

Shelly and Coral laughed.

Then Angel asked, "You're not disappointed, Coral, are you? That you didn't win?"

"Disappointed?" Coral said. "No way! I think one extra book a month is the best prize!"

"She *did* win," Shelly said. "First place isn't the only way to win something."

"In fact, I get my prize *and* I get to take my poster home," Coral said. "That's two wins in my book!"

The girls laughed.

Then someone said, "Can I join you?"

Angel turned. "Cyane!" she said. "Of course you can."

"Congratulations, Cyane!" Shelly said.

"Your poster was great," Coral added.

"Thank you," Cyane replied. "Yours was beautiful, too. Ms. Harbor said the votes were really close. That's why I came over to talk to you." She turned to Angel. "Thank you for making sure the contest was fair, Angel. If you hadn't hurried to share the uncounted ballots, there might have been different winners."

Angel shrugged. "It was the right thing to do. I wish I had done it sooner."

"But you *did* do it," Cyane said. "So thank you. Thank you all for being thoughtful today." She held out her paw. "I know Angel thought my beads were purr-ty. Since my bracelet is broken,

I was wondering if each of you would want one?"

Angel, Shelly, and Coral smiled. "That's so nice of you!" Coral exclaimed.

"We'll add them to our bracelets," Shelly added. "They'll remind us of you!"

"And," Angel purred, "they'll remind us of this wonderful shell-ebration. And the day we all won a prize."

"What prize?" Shelly asked.

Angel grinned. "We all got a new friend!"

The purrmaids have lots of friends around the ocean!

Read on for a sneak peek!

Early one morning in Seadragon Bay, a young mermicorn named Sirena could not sleep. She pushed the curtain on her window open. It was still dark outside! No one else in the Cheval family would be awake yet.

Sirena fluffed her pillow. She pulled the blanket over her head. But she kept tossing and turning. *I'm too excited to sleep,* she thought. *What if today is the day?*

It was the first day of the season. For most mermicorns, that was just another day. But for all the colts and fillies in Seadragon Bay, it was special. That was when the Mermicorn Magic Academy invited new students to the school.

Magic was a part of mermicorn life. But like everything else, magic had to be learned. The best place for that was the Magic Academy. "I hope they pick me today!" Sirena whispered to herself. She finally gave up on sleeping. She floated out of bed and started to get dressed.

Sirena found her lucky blue top and put it on. She brushed out her long rainbow mane. She put on her favorite crystal earrings. Then she peeked out the window again. She could see some sunlight. *It's early,* she thought, *but maybe the mail is already here?*

Sirena swam toward the front door. She tried to be as quiet as a jellyfish. She didn't want to wake her family. But when she passed the kitchen, she saw that her parents were already up!

"Why are you awake?" Sirena asked.

Mom laughed. "Is that how you say good morning?"